Daniel's
Mystery
Egg

Daniel's Mystery Egg

Alma Flor Ada

Illustrated by G. Brian Karas

Green Light Readers
Harcourt, Inc.
San Diego   New York   London

To Daniel, with hugs and kisses
—Abuelita

www.harcourt.com

First Green Light Readers edition 2001
Green Light Readers is a trademark of Harcourt, Inc.,
registered in the United States of America and/or other jurisdictions.

Library of Congress Cataloging-in-Publication Data
Ada, Alma Flor.
Daniel's mystery egg/by Alma Flor Ada; illustrated by G. Brian Karas.
p. cm.
"Green Light Readers."
Summary: When he finds an egg, Daniel and his friends try to guess what is inside.
[1. Eggs—Fiction.] I. Karas, G. Brian ill. II. Title. III. Green Light reader.
PZ7.A1857Dan 2000
[E]—dc21   00-9728
ISBN 0-15-216231-3
ISBN 0-15-216237-2 (pb)

C E G H F D B
A C E G H F D B (pb)

Printed in Mexico

Daniel found a surprise.
It was a small white egg.
He put it in a little box.

Daniel ran to tell Alex. "Look! This is the best egg ever! What could it be?"

"Maybe it will be an ostrich with a long neck!" said Alex.

"You can take it to school for show-and-tell. I can help you."

"I won't need help," said Daniel.
"I think a small animal will come
out of this egg."

Next, Meg came to look.
"Daniel found this egg," said Alex.
"What could it be?"

"Maybe it will be an alligator with big teeth!" said Meg.

"Alligators are not good pets. Maybe you will have to move out of your house. You can all move in with me!"

"We won't need to move," said Daniel.
"I think a nice animal will come out
of this egg."

Next, Tammy came to look.
"Daniel found an egg!" said Meg.
"What could it be?"

"Maybe it will be a duck that quacks all the time!" said Tammy.

"Your house will be very noisy. You will have to teach the duck to quack softly. I can help you."

"I don't think the house will be noisy," said Daniel. "I think a quiet animal will come out of this egg."

"Well, Daniel," said Alex, "what will this small, nice, quiet animal be?"
"We'll have to wait and see," said Daniel.

So they waited, and waited,
and waited....

And then…

One day the egg hatched!

"It doesn't have a long neck," said Alex.
"It doesn't have big teeth," said Meg.
"It doesn't have a noisy quack,"
said Tammy.

"No," said Daniel. "But it IS small, nice, and quiet. It's the best lizard ever!"

Meet the Author and Illustrator

Alma *Ada*

Brian Karas

Alma Flor Ada learned to read out in the garden. Her grandmother taught her by writing the names of plants in the dirt. Even now, Alma Flor Ada's favorite place to read and write is outdoors. Many of her stories are about animals and nature.

Brian Karas used to live in Arizona. There he saw lots of lizards like Daniel's. Brian made the pictures for this story in an interesting way. First he glued bits of colored paper on white paper. Then he painted pictures on this background. "Sometimes I tear up my old artwork and use it in my collages," he says. "I hope you'll try making and painting collages, too. It's fun!"